This book belongs to:

_____

_____

My Mermaid Treasury

My Mermaid Treasury

Produced for Woolworths plc
242–246 Marylebone Road,
London, NW1 6JL
www.woolworths.co.uk

ISBN 978-1-4054-8873-0
Printed in China

Contents

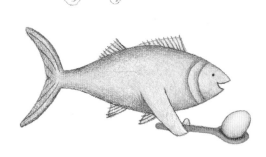

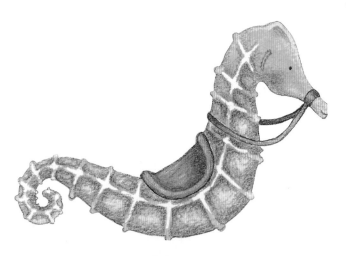

The Little Mermaid

Long ago, deep below the ocean blue, there lay the kingdom of the mer-people. The mer-people were similar to humans but instead of legs they had tails like fish. At the centre of the kingdom stood the mer-king's splendid palace. Inside the palace lived the mer-king, his mother and his six mermaid daughters. The six princesses were all beautiful but the youngest was the fairest of them all. She was also blessed with the sweetest of voices.

The little mermaid loved to hear about the human world. She would spend many hours listening to her grandmother's stories about sailors and their huge ships, about busy towns and animals that walked on the land.

"When you are fifteen," said her grandmother, "you will be allowed to go to the surface of the sea and see all these things for yourself."

Year after year, the little mermaid looked on as her sisters reached their fifteenth birthday. One by one, each mermaid made her first journey to the water's surface.

At last, the little mermaid's fifteenth birthday arrived. As she rose to the water's surface she saw a large ship at anchor. Its decks were alive with men dancing and singing noisily. Among the men was a handsome prince.

It was his sixteenth birthday and the whole ship was celebrating.

The little mermaid watched the handsome prince late into the night. Then the ocean began to bubble and swirl. A storm arrived and the big ship was tossed from wave to wave.

Suddenly, the ship was thrown onto its side and began to sink. The little mermaid realized that the men were in danger but it was so dark that she could not see what was happening. As the ship plunged below the waves, the little mermaid spotted the unconscious body of the prince. Ignoring the danger, she swam to his side and caught hold of him.

The mermaid swam and swam until she reached the nearest shore. She dragged the prince onto a sandy beach and then slipped back into the sea and waited.

Early the next morning, a group of young girls came out of a large white building by the beach to walk along the water's edge. Before long, one of the younger girls found the prince. She knelt beside him as he began to wake up. How the little mermaid's heart ached as the prince smiled up at the young girl. He thought it was she, and not the little mermaid, who had saved him. The little mermaid felt so sad that she plunged beneath the waves and returned home.

Day by day, the little mermaid became more and more unhappy. At last, she revealed her secret to one of her sisters. Soon all the other mermaids knew her story.

Luckily, one of them knew where the prince lived and was happy to show the little mermaid the way to his palace by the sea.

After the little mermaid had found her prince's palace, she used to return there most evenings. Hidden by darkness, she would watch him from the water as he stood on his balcony overlooking the sea. The prince grew more and more dear to the little mermaid. However, she knew that he could never love her, for to be admired by a human she needed two legs instead of a tail.

One day, the little mermaid decided she would risk everything to win the prince's love. So she went to visit an evil witch.

"I know what you want," cackled the witch. "I will prepare you a drink that will give you legs instead of a tail. However, whenever you walk it will feel as if you are walking on broken glass.

Do you agree to this?"

"Yes!" cried the princess.

"If the prince marries another, your heart will break and you will turn into foam on the sea," added the witch. "It will be as if you never existed. Also, you must pay me with your voice."

"But how will I charm the prince without my voice?" asked the little mermaid.

"What do I care?" cried the witch. So the little mermaid gave away her voice in return for the witch's potion. Unable to speak or sing, she headed to the prince's palace. Once there, she drank the witch's potion. She felt it run through her body like sharp knives and then she fell down in a swoon.

When the little mermaid awoke, her tail had been replaced with legs. She stood up to walk and found that the witch had been right – every step felt as if she was walking on broken glass.

However, when she came across the prince, she forgot her pain. The prince asked the little mermaid who she was but, of course, she could not speak.

The prince was delighted with the little mermaid and took her with him everywhere he went. However, he looked upon her as a sweet child and never thought of making her his wife. He would tell her how he wished to marry a young girl who had saved his life after a shipwreck. "I saw her only once," he would say, "but she is the only one I can ever love. She is the girl I wish to marry." The little mermaid was unable to tell him that she was the one who had saved his life.

One day, the prince's parents arranged for him to sail to a neighbouring kingdom to marry a princess. "Don't worry," he told the mermaid. "I must go but it is impossible for me to love her. If I cannot have the girl I love, I will marry you."

However, when the prince saw the princess, he cried out, "It is her! She is the one who saved my life." It was decided that they should marry without delay.

The little mermaid was very sad. As she watched the prince and his bride marry, she wept silent tears. Later, after everyone else was asleep, her sisters appeared. They had lost their beautiful golden hair, and their heads were shaved bare.

"We have made a deal with the witch," said the eldest sister. "We have given her our hair in return for this knife. If you plunge it into the prince's heart, you will become a mermaid again."

The little mermaid loved the prince so dearly that she could never think of taking his life. Throwing the knife aside, she leapt into the ocean. However, instead of dissolving into foam, she found herself floating gently upwards. Around her were many beautiful wispy shapes. Then she saw that she too was like them. The little mermaid had been so sweet and good that she had earned herself a place in heaven.

Susie and the Mermaid

Today was Susie's birthday. Mum and Dad had given her a pretty sea-blue dress and shoes to match.

"Can I try them on now?" she asked.

"Of course, but don't get them dirty," warned her mum. Susie tried on the dress and shoes. They shimmered just like a mermaid's tail. Susie had always wanted to be a mermaid. She wandered down to Mermaid Rock and gazed out to sea, dreaming of what it would be like to be a mermaid.

"I'll make a birthday wish," thought Susie to herself. She closed her eyes. "I wish I could be a mermaid."

When she opened her eyes, she was no longer wearing her birthday dress – she had a mermaid's tail! Susie couldn't believe her luck! Her birthday wish had come true.

But then Susie heard someone crying. She looked around. There was someone sitting on the other side of Mermaid Rock wearing a blue dress just like Susie's new birthday dress!

"Why are you crying?" Susie asked the little girl.

"I'm crying because I've lost my tail," she replied. "You see, I'm a mermaid. But without my tail I can't go home!" As the mermaid cried, her tears splashed into the sea.

Susie suddenly realized what had happened. Her birthday wish must have made her swap places with the mermaid. Susie told the mermaid about her birthday wish.

"What can I do to change us back again?" asked Susie.

"If you can collect my tears from the sea, then you could wish again," said the mermaid.

Susie slipped into the sea. The water didn't feel a bit cold now that she was a mermaid. With her strong new tail she swam quickly to the bottom of the sea. But Susie didn't have any idea how to look for the mermaid's tears!

Susie asked the sea creatures to help her search for the tears. Crabs and fish, lobsters and winkles peered into holes and lifted up stones but it was no use. They couldn't find a single tear. Susie didn't know what to do!

Then she heard, "One-two-three, one-two-three..." and out from an underwater cave danced a large octopus wearing a long string of pearls! Its eight long arms whirled around as the octopus danced and twirled.

"Hello, little mermaid!" said the octopus.

"Can you help me?" asked Susie. "I'm looking for mermaid tears. But I don't know where to start."

"Ah! Well, these pearls are just what you are looking for!" said the octopus. "That's what happens to mermaid tears you know – they turn into pearls! You can have them if you help me take them off!" laughed the octopus.

"Oh, thank you so much!" cried Susie, untangling the pearls.

"Farewell, little mermaid!" laughed the octopus as it danced away, singing, "One-two-three, one-two-three..."

"Goodbye!" Susie smiled, holding the pearls tightly in her hand.

Susie swam back to Mermaid Rock as quickly as she could with the pearls. The mermaid was overjoyed. Susie closed her eyes and wished again. Instantly, she was wearing her blue dress and the mermaid had her tail back.

"Thank you, Susie," said the mermaid. "I hope I'll see you again."

Susie waved goodbye as the mermaid slipped into the sea and swam away. Susie hurried home for her birthday tea. She glanced down at her new blue dress to make sure it was still clean. Around the dress were sewn lots of tiny tear-shaped pearls!

The Lonely Mermaid

There once lived a mermaid named Miriam who was very lonely. All day long she sat on a rock combing her long, yellow hair and singing to herself. Sometimes she would flick her beautiful turquoise fish tail in the water and watch the ripples spreading far out to sea.

Miriam had not always been lonely. In fact, she had once had a pair of playmates called Octopus and Dolphin. Octopus had gone off to another part of the ocean to work for the Sea King. He was always much in demand because he could do eight jobs at once – one with each arm. Dolphin, meanwhile, had gone away to teach singing in a school of dolphins. Miriam once thought she heard his lovely song far away across the ocean and she hoped in vain that he might come back and play.

One day Miriam was sitting on her favourite rock as usual. "How lonely I am," she sighed to her reflection as she combed her hair and gazed at herself in the mirror.

To her astonishment, her reflection seemed to answer back. "Don't be lonely," said a voice. "Come and play with me."

Miriam couldn't understand it at all. She peered into the mirror and then she saw, beyond her own reflection, another mermaid! She was so startled that she dropped the mirror and her comb and spun round.

Miriam was puzzled by the sight in front of her. For there, sitting on the next rock was another mermaid – and yet she didn't look like a mermaid in many ways.

She had short, dark, curly hair and wore a strange costume that definitely wasn't made of seaweed. When Miriam looked down to where the mermaid's fish tail should have been, she wanted to burst out laughing.

For instead of a beautiful tail, the other mermaid had two strange limbs like an extra long pair of arms stretching down.

The other 'mermaid', who was really a little girl called Georgie, was equally amazed by the sight of Miriam. She had seen pictures of mermaids in books before but now she couldn't quite believe her eyes. For here, on the rock beside her, was a real live mermaid!

For a moment they were both too astonished to speak. Then they both said at once, "Who are you?"

"I'm Miriam," said Miriam.

"I'm Georgie," said Georgie.

"Let's go for a swim," said Miriam. Soon the two of them were in the water, chasing each other and giggling.

"Let's play tag along the beach," suggested Georgie, and started swimming towards the shore. She had quite forgotten that Miriam would not be able to run around on dry land. Miriam followed though she was rather afraid, as her mother had always told her not to go near the shore in case she got stranded. Georgie ran out of the water and up on to the beach.

"Wait for me!" called Miriam, struggling in the water as her tail thrashed about. Then, to her astonishment, something strange happened. She found she could leave the water with ease and, looking down, saw that her tail had disappeared and that in its place were two of those strange long arm things like Georgie's.

"What's happened?" she wailed.

Georgie looked round. "You've grown legs!" she shouted in amazement. "Now you can play tag!"

Miriam found that she rather liked having legs. She tried jumping in the air and Georgie taught her to hop and skip.

"You can come and stay at my house but first I must find you some clothes," said Georgie, looking at Miriam. "Wait for me here!"

Georgie ran off and soon she was back with a T-shirt and shorts. Miriam put them on. They ran back to Georgie's house together. "This is my friend Miriam," said Georgie to her mother. "Can she stay for tea?"

"Why, of course," said Georgie's mother.

"What's that strange thing?" whispered Miriam.

"It's a chair," said Georgie. She showed Miriam how to sit on the chair.

All through teatime Miriam watched Georgie to see how she should eat from a plate and drink from a cup and saucer. She'd never tasted food like this before. How she wished she could have chocolate cake at home under the sea!

After tea Miriam said, "Now I'll show you how to do something." Taking Georgie by the hand she led her down to the beach again. There they picked up shells and then Miriam showed Georgie how to make a lovely necklace from shells threaded with seaweed. While they made their necklaces, Miriam taught Georgie how to sing songs of the sea.

Soon it was bedtime. "You can sleep in the spare bed in my room," said Georgie. Miriam slipped in between the sheets. How strange it felt! She was used to feeling water all around her and here she was lying in a bed. She tossed and turned, feeling hotter and hotter, and couldn't sleep at all.

In the middle of the night Miriam got up and threw open the window to get some fresh air. She could smell the salty sea air and she began to feel rather homesick. Then she heard a familiar sound from far away. It was Dolphin calling to her!

The noise was getting closer and closer until at last Miriam knew what she must do. She slipped out of the house and ran down to the beach in the moonlight. As soon as her toes touched the water, her legs turned back into a fish tail and she swam out to sea to join Dolphin.

The next morning, when Georgie woke up, she was very upset to find that her friend had gone. When she told her mother who Miriam really was, her mother said, "The sea is a mermaid's true home and that's where she belongs. But I'm sure you two will always be friends."

And indeed, from time to time, Georgie was sure that she could see Miriam waving to her from the sea.

The Mermaid Fair

Jamie loved diving and he was very good at it. He loved to dive for shellfish and sponges but mainly he loved to look for pearls. Pearls are jewels of the sea and he collected even the tiniest one.

One day Jamie was diving when he saw a sign on a rock. Jamie was very surprised. He swam closer and was even more surprised to read the words: MERMAID FAIR TODAY!

Jamie had heard of mermaids, of course. But he'd never seen one! Jamie took a huge gulp of air and swam towards the fair. He hid behind a rock and watched.

Jamie could hardly believe his eyes; there was a crowd of mermaids having fun at the fair. Some were riding dolphins, some were swimming in races and some were playing games at the stalls. And there were pearls! There was a stall where you could win a pearl by throwing a hoop over it.

At another stall there was a machine where you pulled a special lever and if you saw three shells in a row, a hundred white pearls came out of a hole at the bottom! Two of the mermaids noticed Jamie watching and came over to him.

"You're a strange sort of fish!" teased the fair-haired mermaid.

"I think it must be a boy!" laughed the dark-haired mermaid.

"Hello," said Jamie. To Jamie's amazement, he found he could talk and breathe under water! "Can I take part in your fair? I'd love to win some pearls!"

"Oh, you don't want boring old pearls," said one.

"What you really want are these," and she opened her hand to show Jamie a plastic comb! It was a pink plastic comb with a flower on it. The mermaid had found it one day in a rock pool. She thought it was the most beautiful thing she had ever seen. Jamie told her he would bring her plenty of combs if she would show him how to win a pearl.

"That's easy!" she told him. "You just have to win the dolphin race!" So Jamie entered the dolphin race. But it was not as easy as he thought. He found that dolphins are very slippery to ride, and jumping through a hoop under water is impossible. Unless, of course, you are a mermaid!

It was nearly time to go and Jamie had not won a single prize! At the very last stall there was the biggest pearl he had ever seen. It was huge – almost as big as a coconut. The mermaids showed Jamie what to do. He had to throw a sponge at the pearl to knock it over. Jamie couldn't believe his luck! If there was one thing he could do, it was throw a sponge.

The mermaids gathered round Jamie to cheer him on.

He had one or two near misses and then, amidst lots of laughter, he knocked the huge pearl off the stand with his third try.

"You've won!" the mermaids shouted excitedly. "The pearl is yours!"

Jamie swam back to his boat, delighted. The next day he returned clutching a box filled with pretty plastic combs. When the mermaids saw them they danced for joy in the waves and kissed him on both cheeks. After that Jamie saw the mermaids whenever he went diving and he always took them a special plastic comb.

The Naughty Mermaids

Of all the mermaids that lived in the sea, Jazz and Cassandra were the naughtiest. They were not supposed to swim above sea when there were people about. But their latest prank was to swim to the lighthouse and call out to the little boy who lived there.

"Coo-ee!" they would call and, when the little boy looked towards them, they giggled and dived under the waves.

"Coo-ee!" they called again from the other side of the lighthouse. Just as he ran round to see them, they dived under the waves again!

When King Neptune heard about it, he was very cross indeed!

"I won't have this naughty behaviour," he boomed. "Mermaids should not mix with children!"

But Jack, that was the boy's name, was lonely at the lighthouse. There was no one to play with. One day, Jack's mum made him a picnic. Jack laid the food on a cloth on the rocks. He had pizza and crisps and fizzy drink and chocolate.

The two naughty mermaids popped up from the waves. They soon spotted all the food.

"Hello!" they called to Jack. "Are you going to eat all this food by yourself?"

Jack was so surprised that he couldn't speak. He'd never seen the mermaids before.

"Yes," said Jack, at last. "I mean, no! You can have some of my picnic, if you like."

The mermaids had never had pizza or crisps or fizzy drink or chocolate before. They ate so much they felt quite sick! They swam home slowly, hoping King Neptune wouldn't spot them. But he did! And he summoned them to come and see him.

"Be warned!" said King Neptune. "Mermaids are not like children. They cannot behave like children and they cannot eat the food that children eat!"

For a while Jazz and Cassandra played with the other ocean creatures and ate mermaid food, like shrimps and seaweed. But they soon became bored!

"I'm longing for some pizza," said Jazz to Cassandra one day.

"So am I," answered Cassandra, "and some of those crispy things."

"Mmmm, and fizzy stuff!"

"And chocolate!"

The naughty mermaids looked at each other. Then, holding hands they swam up to the surface.

Jack was waiting for them with a picnic all ready. They ate and ate and ate. It all tasted so good. Afterwards they played hide-and-seek in the waves while Jack ran round the lighthouse, trying to spot them. The mermaids enjoyed themselves so much, they came back the next day and the next.

On the third day, the mermaids said goodbye and started to swim to the bottom of the sea. But, oh dear! Their tails had become stiff and heavy. They could not move! King Neptune was right! Mermaids can't behave like children. They clung onto the rocks around the lighthouse and began to cry.

"What's wrong?" shouted Jack, alarmed.

"We're not supposed to eat children's food," they told him.

Jack knew exactly what to do! He got his net and bucket and searched the island, collecting shrimps and seaweed from the rock pools.

For three days and three nights he fed the mermaids proper mermaid food. By the end of the third day they could move their tails again and swim.

When they arrived home King Neptune was waiting for them. This time, King Neptune wasn't angry – he was glad to see them back safely.

"I hope you have learned a lesson," he said, quite gently. "Jack has been a good friend so you can play with him again. As long as you don't eat his food!"

From then on they saw quite a lot of their friend Jack, often going up to talk and play with him. But they never again ate Jack's food, except sometimes they had a piece of chocolate!

The Fantastic Seahorse Race

It was a normal day in the Enchanted City. Mermaids and mermen went about their business as usual. Suddenly there was a distant rumbling and within seconds a whirlwind had hit the streets! The water swirled in every direction – hats went flying and one little mermaid lost her balance completely and fell on her bottom.

A great cry of "Wahoooooo!" rose and then vanished into the distance as the disturbance passed.

"It's that Emmy racing her seahorses again!" cried an old couple, shaking their fists after her.

The King's messenger finally caught up with Emmy Mermaid and summoned her to the King.

"Now Emmy, I will not have this wahooing through my streets!" he said sternly. "I've racked my brains for the perfect punishment and I'm putting YOU in charge of the celebrations for the Enchanted City Day!" Then he smiled to himself and thought, "That should keep her quiet for a while!"

Emmy went to complain to her friend Pearl.

"Enchanted City Day is the most important holiday of our year!" she wailed. "What am I going to do?"

"Let's think," said Pearl. "What was the King punishing you for?"

"Riding my seahorses too fast in the street," grumbled Emmy.

"That's it!" cried Pearl. "You should hold a race!"

Soon everyone was talking about the Great Seahorse Race.

"I bet I win," cried Charlie. "I'm really fast."

"You haven't even got a seahorse to ride," said Buster Blowfish sensibly.

"Well, I'll borrow one. Emmy's got lots."

"I never learned to ride," said Tommy Tuna sadly, "and I'm sure I'd fall off."

"You can't fall off," explained Buster patiently. "You're a fish – you'd just float off."

Everyone was going around saying, "I bet I win!" or "I bet Emmy wins!" and soon Charlie had an idea. "Since everyone's SO eager to bet," he announced, "I'm going to make it official. Step right up and place your bets! Only one seashell to place a bet."

"Young man!' said Oscar Octopus, swimming up behind Charlie, who was struggling with a large bag of seashells. "What do you intend to do with all your earnings?"

Charlie looked astonished. "I'm going to buy myself lots of FANTASTIC stuff, of course," he said.

"Oh no, you're not!" said Oscar. "You know the rules. Betting is only allowed if it's for fun or for charity. You can give those seashells to the school in the Enchanted City."

"Do I have to?" grumbled Charlie. But he did as he was told.

The day of the Great Seahorse Race arrived. Everyone flooded to the Enchanted City Racetrack. The contestants were all feeling very nervous.

"I really don't think I should be doing this," trembled Tommy Tuna, looking very pale. Buster secretly felt the same way, but he said, "Don't be silly, it's just for fun."

"I'm going to win!" cried Charlie.

Just then Emmy came storming up to the starting post on a beautiful, sleek horse. Her saddle and bridle were made of silk and she wore a peaked jockey cap. "Everyone ready?" she called cheerfully.

The King dropped the flag and the riders were off! Charlie made a tremendous start but then he seemed to lose his balance and soon he was swimming furiously after his horse. Buster was running a good race.

Scuttle the Crab was clinging furiously to the back of a very old, tired seahorse that really didn't want to be in the race. Sizzle and Slink, the electric eels, shared a horse and seemed to be doing pretty well. Pearl rode side-saddle and looked very pretty, waving to all the spectators.

But Emmy! Emmy rode like the wind. The water swirled and whirled around her and no one had any chance of keeping up. She wasn't even riding the best horse in her stable – she had lent that to Charlie – but she was such a good rider that it didn't make a bit of difference.

She whistled past the finishing line, the flag came down and a cheer went up. "Hurrah for Emmy! The fastest mermaid in town!"

"Well Emmy," said the King with a smile. "It's nice to give you a medal for riding too fast instead of a punishment!"

"Thank you, Your Majesty!" said Emmy.

Then Emmy turned to the crowds. "Food is being served in the pink striped tent!" she announced. The chef waved from the tent where he had been busy all day making a pot of seaweed surprise. "And there are lots of other races!" cried Emmy.

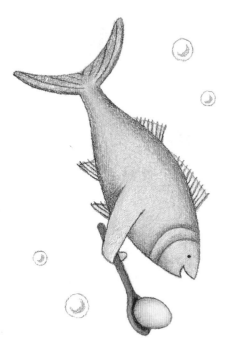

When everyone had had enough to eat and drink, the fun races began. There was an egg-and-spoon race which Tommy Tuna won, much to his astonishment. "But I never win anything!" he protested, looking quite overcome with emotion as the King gave him his medal.

Next there was a sack race. Pearl almost won this race but at the last minute she tripped on a seashell and Charlie beat her to the finishing line.

"Hurrah for me!" cried Charlie. Then he caught sight of Pearl's face. "We'll share the prize," he said promptly. "You would have won if it wasn't for that seashell."

"Well done, my boy!" beamed Oscar Octopus.

Afterwards, there was a cartwheeling race. The King roared with laughter as he watched the fish trying to spin on their fins. No one was any good at it except for Oscar Octopus, who could turn SPECTACULAR cartwheels.

Thanks to his eight arms Oscar covered more ground in a single cartwheel than anyone, so he won the race and was sitting enjoying a glass of seaweed surprise, keeping score and signing autographs by the time the first runner-up arrived at the finishing line.

In the evening, when everyone started to get tired, there were jugglers and plate-spinners and mermaids walking on stilts. There was a clownfish and a crab that made FANTASTIC animals out of balloons. Scuttle was very impressed but afterwards, when he tried to make one himself, his sharp claws kept bursting the balloons.

Finally, there was a big parade. Everyone who had won prizes rode at the front and Emmy Mermaid had pride of place in the King's chariot.

"You've done very well, Emmy," said the King, patting her shoulder. "I'm very proud of you. In the future, perhaps you'll put your energy into organizing fantastic things like this, instead of wasting it by wahooing through my streets!"

Emmy grinned back at him but she made no promises!

Jade and the Jewels

Jade was the prettiest mermaid in the lagoon! Her hair was jet black and reached right down to the tip of her swishy, fishy tail. Her eyes were as green as emeralds and her skin was as white as the whitest pearl. But Jade was so big-headed and vain that the other mermaids didn't like her!

"That Jade thinks too much of herself!" the other mermaids would say. "One of these days she'll come unstuck!"

There was one creature, though, who was fond of Jade and that was Gentle, the giant turtle. He followed her wherever she went.

But Jade didn't even notice Gentle. She lived in a world of her own. She spent all her time combing her hair and admiring her reflection in the mirror.

One day Jade overheard the mermaids talking about a pirate ship that had sunk to the bottom of the ocean. On board was a treasure chest filled with precious jewels.

"But no one dares take the jewels," whispered the mermaids, "because the pirate ship is cursed!"

"I'm going to find that pirate ship," Jade told Gentle, "and the treasure chest!"

"But what about the curse?" asked Gentle.

"Oh, never mind that. Just imagine how beautiful I will look wearing all those jewels!" said Jade and right away she set off.

"Wait for me!" called Gentle, paddling after her. "It's too dangerous to go alone!"

Jade swam to a deep part of the ocean she had never been to before. She dived through shoals of colourful fish, past the edge of the coral reef and deep, deep down to the very bottom of the ocean.

Finally, they found the shipwreck.

"Be careful, Jade," said Gentle. "Remember there is a curse on this pirate wreck."

"Nonsense," Jade told him. "I've come to get the jewels and I'm not going home without them!"

Jade searched the wreck until she saw the treasure chest through a porthole. Jade swam inside and reached out to touch the chest. The lid sprang open and brilliant jewels spilled over the sides. The colours were dazzling.

Jade lifted out a necklace and put it round her neck. There was a little gold and silver mirror in the chest. She held it up to admire her reflection. The necklace was beautiful! Jade looked lovelier than ever.

Suddenly, there was a loud crack and the mirror shattered! Instantly the necklace turned to stone. It was the ship's curse!

Jade tried to take the necklace off but she couldn't. She tried to swim but the necklace was so heavy she couldn't move.

"Help!" Jade cried out. "Help! Help!" Gentle, the giant turtle, heard her and swam to the porthole.

"Help me, Gentle," she cried. "Please help me!"

"I warned you to be careful," said Gentle.

Jade began to cry. "I should have listened to you, Gentle," she sobbed.

Gentle's powerful flippers broke the necklace and freed Jade. As Jade and Gentle swam away from the wreck, Gentle said, "You don't need fancy jewels, Jade. You're pretty without them."

Once she was safely home, Jade told the other mermaids about the pirate ship curse.

"I've certainly learned my lesson," said Jade. "I'll never be vain again." And, from that day on, they were all friends. But Gentle was always her very best friend of all.

King Neptune's Day off

Trini the little mermaid worked in King Neptune's palace. It was a beautiful palace, with fountains and a statue of King Neptune in the centre of the courtyard. Trini was happy working there. But some fierce sharks guarded the palace.

Today it was King Neptune's birthday. King Neptune called Trini to see him.

"I'm taking the day off," he said. "I'd like you to organize a birthday banquet for me this evening when I come back. So, until then, you will be in charge." And off he went!

The sharks were delighted! They thought they would have some fun while King Neptune was away.

"I'm in charge, so you must do as I say," Trini told them sternly, after the king had left. The sharks just sniggered at her and didn't answer.

71

Trini set to work. She asked a team of fish to collect shrimps and special juicy seaweed. She told the crabs to collect smooth, pearly shells to use as plates. Then she sent her mermaid friends to collect pieces of coral to decorate the tables.

But the sharks were determined to make mischief and spoil everything. Before long they saw the fish carrying a net full of delicious food. "Give us that," they snapped, and in a few gulps the food was gone.

As soon as the crabs came back with their shell plates, the sharks took the shells and began throwing them to each other.

"Stop it at once!" cried Trini. But the sharks ignored her.

Then the sharks spotted the mermaids watching
close by. They started to chase them all around the
courtyard. "Stop it!" cried Trini. But the sharks just
laughed and carried on chasing the mermaids.

Then Trini had an idea. She would trick the sharks!
While they were chasing the mermaids, Trini squeezed
through a crack in the hollow statue of King Neptune.
The sharks were having great fun. The mermaids
dropped all their pretty coral and swam away. The
sharks couldn't stop laughing.

They gathered around King Neptune's statue to plan some more mischief.

Suddenly, a voice like thunder boomed, "Behold, it is I, King Neptune, Emperor of all the Seas and Oceans." The sharks were very frightened.

Then the voice bellowed, "Do as Trini commands or you will be banished from the kingdom!"

Then the voice from inside the statue told the sharks to pick up the plates and fetch more food and lay the tables for the banquet. And, while they were busy, Trini crept out from inside the hollow statue where she had been hiding!

So Trini's banquet was a great success. Everyone was there, even the sharks! But they had to stand guard outside the palace, while everyone inside enjoyed the food, music and dancing. King Neptune had a marvellous time and asked Trini if she would always be his special helper.

"I'd be delighted," she answered, blushing!

The Mermaid in the Pool

Josh and Emily were on holiday at the seaside. Their mum and dad had found an amazing house with a big swimming pool. But, best of all, their bedroom overlooked the beach. It was perfect!

The first night there was a storm. The wind howled. The lightning flashed. The waves crashed over the beach and right up to the house. The children lay in bed listening to the storm.

By morning, the storm was over. The children woke early and looked out of their window. The garden furniture had blown over, there was seaweed all over the lawn and there was a mermaid in the swimming pool!

That's right! There was a mermaid in the swimming pool! The mermaid was swimming up and down the pool. Josh and Emily rushed outside but, when the mermaid saw them coming, she huddled in a corner of the pool. She was frightened.

"I'm sorry I swam into your blue pool," said the mermaid. "I didn't mean any harm!"

"It's okay!" said Emily gently. "We didn't mean to frighten you."

"That's right," said Josh. "We just wanted to meet you. We've never seen a mermaid before."

"My name is Marina," said the mermaid. "I was playing in the sea with my friend Blue, the dolphin, when the storm began. A huge wave washed me in and now I'm stranded and Blue is missing!"

"We'll help you look for Blue," said Emily at once. "We might be able to spot your friend from our bedroom window."

As soon as their mum and dad were safely out of the way, Josh and Emily found a wheelbarrow and wheeled Marina into the house.

"I've only had sky over my head before," said Marina. "The house won't fall on me, will it?"

"Of course not," smiled Josh. They showed Marina all sorts of things she'd never seen before. She thought the moving pictures on the television were weird. She thought Emily's teddy bear was wonderful and that beds were the silliest things she had ever seen!

But, although they looked out of the window, there was no sign of Blue the dolphin in the sea.

"I have to go home soon!" Marina said sadly. "I can't stay out of the water for long and I must find Blue. If only I hadn't lost my shell horn in the storm I could call him."

"We'll take you down to the sea," said Josh.

"And help you look for your shell," said Emily.

They lifted Marina back into the wheelbarrow and pushed her down to the beach. They spent the rest of the day searching for Marina's shell along the seashore. They had almost given up when, suddenly, Emily spotted a large shell half buried in the sand. Josh found a stick and dug it out.

"It's my shell!" cried Marina.

They washed the sand from the shell and Marina blew into it. The most beautiful sound drifted out across the waves. Straight away, there was an answering call! Far out to sea, they saw a streak of blue-grey. It was leaping high over the waves, swimming towards them. It was Blue, the dolphin!

Marina gave a cry of joy and swam to meet him. She flung her arms around his neck and hugged him. Then she turned to the watching children.

"Thank you for helping me," she called.

"See you next year!" called Josh and Emily. And they watched as Marina and Blue swam swiftly and smoothly together, back out to sea.

Shimmer
and the River

"How many times have I asked you not to wander off?" said Shimmer the Mermaid's mum, as they swam home from a visit to the surface. "You know you're not allowed to go near the river on the beach."

"Why not?" asked Shimmer. "What's wrong with swimming near the river?"

But Shimmer's mother was in too much of a hurry to answer questions. "Not now, Shimmer," she said, impatiently. "Just come along. I'm far too busy to float around arguing with you."

Just then, Swoop the Seagull landed on a large rock nearby.

"YOO-HOO! Swoop, dear!" called Shimmer's mum, flashing through the water with a huge swish of her tail. "I just wanted to have a quick word with you. Have you got a moment?"

"I thought we were in a hurry!" Shimmer muttered, sitting on a ledge. "We'll be here forever now!"

Suddenly the bored little mermaid caught sight of a shoal of angel fish, darting through the water. "How lovely!" she cried, forgetting all about not wandering off. With a flick of her tail, she swam off to play chase with the multi-coloured fish. In and out of the rocks they darted, chasing through underwater archways as they went.

Just when Shimmer had nearly caught them up, the shoal turned in a flash and disappeared into a cave.

"You can't escape!" laughed Shimmer, following them. "I know you're in here!" But there was no sign of the glittering shoal. Shimmer swam deeper and deeper down the cave's tunnels, searching for her friends.

"Stop hiding!" she called, her voice echoing around.

Shimmer began to feel a little worried. It was dark in the tunnel and there was no sign of anyone at all.

"I think it's time I turned back," she said to herself, remembering her mother's warnings. "But which way do I go?" Shimmer tried first one tunnel, then another, but none of them seemed to lead in the direction of home. She was lost!

"I'll just have to choose one tunnel and go for it!" she decided, swimming off down one that seemed a little brighter than the rest. "This one has to come out somewhere!"

Shimmer had been swimming for what seemed like ages when she began to notice something strange. As the light at the end of the tunnel got brighter, the water began to get warmer – and it tasted rather funny, too. There was no salt in it!

Finally, she popped out at the end of the tunnel in a large still pool. Shimmer rubbed her eyes in amazement. This pool was like no other she had ever seen. There was no yellow sand or seaweed in sight.

Instead, the edge of the silver pool was soft velvety green, with strange plants growing all around it.

"I must have come out in the river!" she gasped, gazing about her. "How beautiful it all is. I wonder why we're not allowed to come here!"

Just then, Shimmer heard a loud cough and turned round to see a large green frog sitting on a nearby rock. "You're very unusual for a fish!" it croaked.

"But I'm not a fish!" exclaimed Shimmer in surprise. "I'm a mermaid. I live in the ocean!"

"In the ocean!" exclaimed the frog, grinning from ear to ear. "How wonderful to meet someone from the OCEAN!" Then he gave a very loud croak. Slowly, all sorts of woodland creatures began to peep out from behind the bushes to say hello.

"They ran and hid when they first saw you," chuckled the frog. "We've never seen a mermaid before! Please will you tell us all about life in the ocean?"

So Shimmer began to describe her home to the animals. She told them about the games of chase she played with the fish, about the friendly dolphins, the grumpy crabs and lobsters, about the beautiful coral reef and the sea anemones that lived on it.

She was so busy talking to her new friends that she didn't notice a shadow swooping over the pond. Suddenly, there was a loud splash as Swoop the Seagull landed in the water beside her.

"Thank goodness I've found you!" squawked the gull. "We must leave immediately! Hurry! I will show you the shortcut back to the ocean."

"It's not fair!" said Shimmer crossly. "I don't want to go home yet. I bet Mum sent you to fetch me!"

Swoop looked very serious. "Yes, she did," he said. "And it's a very good job she did, too. Mermaids become ill if they stay in water without salt for too long. If you don't believe me, look at your scales!"

Sure enough, Shimmer's once-glittering scales were colourless and dull.

"That's why your mum warned you not to swim off," said Swoop, "and why you're not allowed to swim in the river."

Shimmer stroked her grey tail, sadly. "I'm sorry, Swoop," she apologized, looking shame-faced. "I didn't mean to cause so much trouble. From now on I'll try and listen to what Mum says. It's just that I've made lots of new friends here, and now I won't be able to keep in touch with them!"

Swoop looked around at all the woodland creatures gathered by the pond and thought carefully for a moment. "Don't worry!" he squawked. "I can deliver messages for you. I often pass this way."

Shimmer and the woodland animals were delighted at the suggestion.

"We can send each other news by Seagull Post!" laughed Shimmer, waving goodbye to her new friends. Then, with a flick of her tail, she disappeared beneath the water and headed back to the salty ocean, where mermaids belong.

The End